ARE YOU AN EV?

Discover all the great things EVs can do!

Are You an EV?
Discover all the great things EVs can do!

Published by Ideanomics, Inc.

1441 Broadway, Suite 5116
New York, NY 10018
212-206-1216

ideanomics.com

Copyright © 2022 Ideanomics

Art by Kat Hayashida
Story by Natasha Overin
Edited by Namson Pham
Designed by Sela Foster

ISBN: 978-1-66786-792-2

"Within each of us is the innate ability to change the world for the better, so long as we believe in the power of our dreams."

Alf Poor, Ideanomics CEO

Evita was different from other cars in her city.
She was the only one powered by electricity.

To be all alone is sometimes quite sad,
And that's what Evita told her granddad.

"Evita, you can do everything and even much MORE.
There's a whole world of EVs for you to explore."

She took her grandfather's advice as an opportunity cue,
To go find what great things EVs can do.

She didn't travel too far before she saw a van on the road
That didn't have a tailpipe from which exhaust flowed.

"ARE YOU AN EV?" she asked with no hesitation,
The van answered proudly, with a mirror rotation.

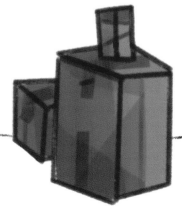

"I'm Victor the van, an EV delivery solution,
I've got no emissions and I make no pollution."

Victor and Evita set off to look for more clues,
to find more great things EVs can do.

Evita saw a scooter and
shouted with glee,

"Excuse me!
"ARE YOU AN EV?"

"I'm Suri the scooter, an EV on two wheels,
I'm small and I'm fast, and I'm delivering meals."

Suri, Victor, and Evita, set off as a crew,
to find more great things EVs can do.

On the road something passed them as quick as the wind,
a red-painted blur with a real fast wheel spin.

When they caught up at the next traffic light,
"ARE YOU AN EV?" Evita asked with delight.

"I'm Mika the motorcycle. I'm an EV sport bike!
And if you're touring with me well, what's not to like?"

"I've got instantaneous torque, so I accelerate quick,
that means I go from 0 to 60 lickety-split!"

From New York to Detroit,
hundreds of miles they speeded.

Rest and recharge
was just what they needed.

The station had charging plugs all around.
There were even big pads
that could charge from the ground!

The big pad was taken up by a bus,
"ARE YOU AN EV?" Evita asked to discuss.

"I'm Blair the bus. I'm public EV transportation,
I take all kinds of people from station to station!"

"I drive all day without rest on my route,
and I charge wirelessly while I'm out and about."

Blaire, Mika, Suri, Victor, and Evita, set out anew,
to find more great things EVs can do.

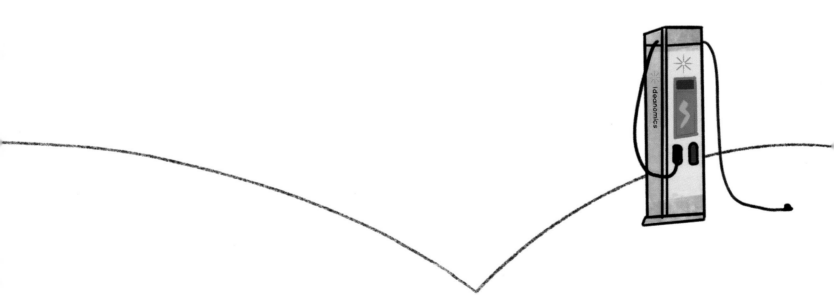

They saw a truck hauling a big load with ease.
"Hello!" said Evita. **"ARE YOU AN EV?"**

"I'm Trayton the Truck, and I'm a Hybrid EV
that's best in my class.
I run on both electricity and natural gas!"

"I can travel up to a thousand miles per fill.
Efficient and clean, I save on the bills."

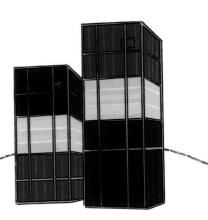

Trayton, Blaire, Mika, Suri, Victor, and Evita,
the assembly grew,
to find more great things EVs can do.

The six friends decided to stop at a park,
and there they saw something that made quite a mark.

A four-wheeled vehicle was planting a tree.
"ARE YOU AN EV?" Evita asked, in her glee.

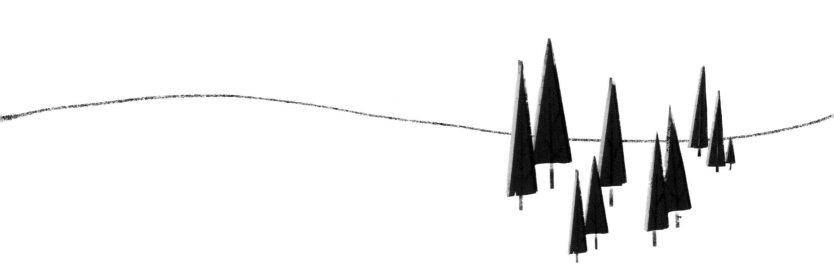

"I do all the work with no noise and no fumes,
I don't disturb or pollute the things humans consume."

It was time to go home, so Evita bid her new friends "adieu,"
she learned many great things EVs can do!

Evita came home with a new kind of mood,
the little EV had new fortitude.

Everyone can have sisters and brothers,
it just takes investment and time to find others.

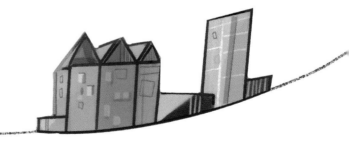

Her travels had taught her that "different" was good.
What mattered was what you had under the hood.

A Special Thanks

To the entire Ideanomics family worldwide committed to accelerating the commercial adoption of electric vehicles every day.